# PINGU
## and the Letter

BBC CHILDREN'S BOOKS

Pingu was feeling hungry. He had been playing outside with his friends and had decided to come back home for a snack.

Pingu had a quick look round for something to eat
and spotted an interesting-looking letter on the table.

"I wonder who that's for," he said to himself.

But Pingu couldn't read the writing
on the envelope.

"It's probably something
boring for Dad," he decided.

3

He put the letter down and went to look for some
food. There, on the dresser, were three lovely
doughnuts. They were just what Pingu felt like eating.
He had  a quick look round to check that no one
was about and then . . .

. . . he tossed a doughnut up in the air, caught it in his mouth and gobbled it up as quickly as he could.

"These are yummy," said
Pingu to himself and he
tucked into the other two
doughnuts on the plate.

6

"That's better," said Pingu. He was about to go back outside to play when he remembered the letter.
"I'll open the envelope and have a quick look at it," he told himself. "No one will know."

Pingu had just started to take out the letter when he heard a noise outside the front door. It was Mum and Pinga coming back from doing the shopping.

"Oh, no!" gasped Pingu. "I mustn't let them see that I've opened the letter!"

Pingu began to panic. He knew Mum would be furious if she found out what he had done. Pingu's dad was a postman and it was a rule that you never opened letters that weren't addressed to you.

"Help!" he whimpered. "What can I do?"

Pingu hadn't any time to think. Mum and Pinga were about to come in. Quickly, he stuffed the envelope under a cushion just as he heard the front door open.

In burst Pinga looking very excited.

"Hello, Pingu!" she shouted. "Mum and I have just been shopping."

Mum came in after Pinga, carrying a large bunch
of flowers.

"Hello, Pingu!" she said, smiling.

Then Mum saw Pingu's anxious face. "Are you all
right?" she asked.

"I'm fine," Pingu replied in a squeaky, nervous voice. He was trying hard not to look guilty, but he couldn't stop himself from glancing at the cushion where he'd hidden the envelope.

Suddenly Mum noticed something.
"Where's that letter gone?" she cried.
"I left it on the table when we went
out. Have you seen it, Pingu?"
    Pingu shook his head glumly.

Mum and Pinga began to search around the room. "That's very odd," muttered Mum. "It must be here somewhere."

Pingu watched them both nervously.

It wasn't long before Pinga came looking near the chair where Pingu had hidden the envelope. Pingu shooed her away.

"You won't find that stupid old letter here," he said, crossly.

"What are you hiding?" asked Pinga, suspiciously.

"I'm not hiding anything," said Pingu, barring her way. "Just go and look somewhere else."

"Bossy-boots," said Pinga and she stuck her tongue out at him.

All at once there was a cry from Mum.
"Where on earth are the doughnuts
I bought?" she exclaimed. "Everything
seems to be going missing today!"
Pingu looked guilty, but he didn't
say anything.

Pinga was determined to find the letter. She was
sure Pingu had hidden it somewhere. She peered
hopefully under his bed, but couldn't see it
anywhere.

"I can't find the letter," Pinga told Mum. "But I'm sure Pingu knows where it is. He won't let me search anywhere near him."

"Won't he?" said Mum. "Well, we'll soon see about that!"

Mum marched over to Pingu.

"Will you please stop wasting our time, Pingu, and give me that letter at once," she said, crossly.

Pingu reached under the cushion and found the letter. Without looking up, he handed it over to Mum.

"I told you so," said Pinga, triumphantly.

Mum opened the letter and burst out laughing.
"It's an invitation for *you*!" she exclaimed.
"For *me*?" said Pingu, amazed.

Pingu took the invitation from Mum and stared at it. He couldn't believe that the letter had been for him, all along.

"It's a birthday party!" he cried. "And it's today!"

"Look," said Pinga. "There's a paper hat for you in the envelope as well!" She tossed it across to Pingu.

"I'm going to the party, too," said Pinga, finding her own party hat. "That's why Mum and I went shopping – to buy some flowers as a birthday present."

"And to think I nearly didn't get to open my own party invitation!" said Pingu.

"I'm glad we're going together, Pingu," squeaked Pinga, excitedly. "We're going to have such fun."

"But the party is this afternoon," cried Pingu,
suddenly. "It starts at three o'clock. We mustn't miss it!"

All three of them looked up at clock. The party was just about to begin.

"Oh, my goodness," cried Mum. "You'd better hurry along there straight away."

Pingu and Pinga rushed off through the snow.
"Don't go too fast, Pingu," whined Pinga. "I can't
keep up!"

They arrived just in time for the party. There were lots of games and then a big birthday tea.

"We only just made it," Pingu cheerfully told his friends. "I won't go hiding party invitations again!"

# More delightful Pingu stories to read and favourite characters to collect

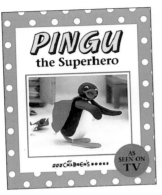

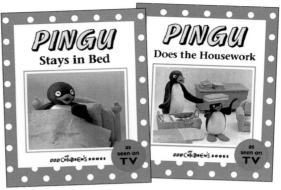

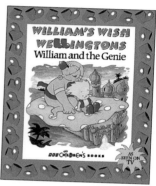

Pingu magazine every month
Make learning fun!

BBC CHILDREN'S PUBLISHING